New Mexico Native Americans

A Kid's Look at Our State's Chiefs, Tribes, Reservations, Powwows, Lore, and More From The Past and the Present

By Carole Marsh

Native American Heritage™

Graphic Design: Lynette Rowe • Cover Design: Victoria DeJoy

Published by
GALLOPADE INTERNATIONAL
800-536-2GET
www.gallopade.com

Gallopade is proud to be a member of these educational organizations and associations:

The National School Supply and Equipment Association (NSSEA)
American Booksellers Association (ABA)
Virginia Educational Media Association (VEMA)
Association of Partners for Public Lands (APPL)
Museum Store Association (MSA)
National Association for Gifted Children (NAGC)
Publishers Marketing Association (PMA)
International Reading Association (IRA)
Association of African American Museums (AAAM)

Native American Heritage™ Series

Native American Big Activity Book

Native American Biographies

Native American Coloring Book

Native American Heritage Book

Native American Timeline

New Mexico State Stuff™

- My First Pocket Guide: New Mexico
- My First Book About New Mexico
- New Mexico Coloring Book
- The Big New Mexico Reproducible Activity Book
- Jeopardy: Answers & Questions About Our State
- New Mexico "Jography!": A Fun Run Through Our State
- New Mexico Gamebooks
- New Mexico Bingo Games
- New Mexico Illustrated Timelines
- New Mexico Project Books
- New Mexico Bulletin Board Set
- New Mexico PosterMap
- New Mexico Stickers
- Let's Discover New Mexico! CD-ROM

Word from the Author

Hello!

I hope you are as interested in North America's wonderful Indian heritage as I am!

Like most kids, I grew up thinking of Indians as the other half of Cowboys. Today, of course, we are getting a much clearer and more accurate picture of what the first peoples on our land were all about. These "facts" are much more fascinating than anything Hollywood can make up. And you probably won't find much of this information in your history textbook!

I am 1/16 Cherokee. This is something I am very proud of and happy about. My grandmother was 1/4 Cherokee. She had tan skin, long gray hair and a very Indian look – especially if I did something bad! Her maiden name was Carrie Corn. Of course, when she got married, she took her husband's name, so it was many years before I learned to appreciate the significance of my native heritage.

Today, I'm trying to make up for lost time by exploring my roots as deeply as I can. One of the most interesting things I've learned is how fascinating all of the Indian tribes are – in the past, the present and future!

As you read about "your" Indians, remember that all native peoples were part of an ever-changing network of time, ideas, power and luck — good and bad. This is certainly a history that is not "dead," but continues to change – often right outside our own back doors! – all the time.

Carole Marsh
She-Who-Writes

PS: Many references show different spellings for the same word. I have tried to select the most common spelling for the time period described. I would not want to be in an Indian spelling bee!

A is for . . .

Adobe

Brick made of mud plus straw and dried in the sun. Houses made of adobe are cool inside, even in high temperatures, because the walls are so thick.

Awl

An Indian's "needle." Often made from wood, thorns, bone, or metal, it was used to punch holes in skins so they could be sewn together.

Atlatl

A throwing device used by prehistoric Indians to hunt deer and antelope. It let them hurl a spear with a deadly force.

Acoma Pueblo

May be the oldest continuously occupied site in the Western Hemisphere. Elevation about 7,000 feet. Established around A.D. 1150.

Anasazi

Commonly used name for a group of early New Mexico people who were ancestors of the Pueblo peoples. The Anasazi were descended from the early Basketmaker peoples of our area. They achieved great progress in the arts, architectural engineering and agriculture. The modern Pueblo peoples object to the use of this term, which in Navajo means "enemy ancestors" and prefer Hisatsinom or Moqui.

Altar

A platform made of rocks or animal skulls; some had bowls, feathers, rattles, or skins on them. Indians prayed at these altars for things like good crops or expert hunting skills.

Arrow

A long, slender shaft made of reed, cane, or wood; pointed tip was attached to one end and split feathers to the other. Feathers helped the arrows fly straight.

Arrowhead

The pointed tip of an arrow, made of bone, antler, wood, or iron. Some tips had barbs that would embed themselves in flesh. These barbs made it difficult for an enemy to remove the arrowhead from a wound.

Apache

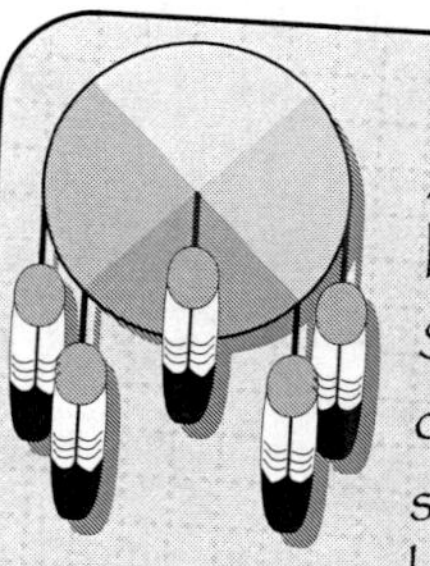

After getting the horse from the Spanish, they quickly became superior horsemen. Got their name from the Zuñi Indians; "apachu" means enemy. Primarily a nomadic tribe that roamed the Southwest, they were best known for raiding before they were put on reservations. They are master coiled basket makers, with a complex mythology and well-defined society.

Aborigine

A member of the earliest known population of a region.

B is for . . .

Band

A subdivision of an Indian tribe. In earlier times, a band was sometimes created when part of a tribe split off from the main group. The band also chose new leadership.

Bells

Pueblo Indians had bells very early; metallic bells may have evolved from the rattle made of shells or clay. Copper bells with stone tinklers have been dug up in New Mexico.

Bonito Pueblo

Anasazi structure in the Chaco Canyon complex. Multiple stories with more than 600 rooms that could house at least 1,000 people.

Bosque Redondo

Reservation near Fort Sumner where the Navajo Indians were forced to march to during the winter of 1864. The resettlement and forced labor of the Apache and Navajo were a disaster. The land could not produce enough food for the thousands of Indians living here. More than 2,000 Indians died of starvation and disease. In 1868, the federal government agreed that the forced resettlement had been a failure. They granted the Navajos 3.5 million acres of reservation lands in their traditional homeland in the Four Corners region.

Baskets

Made from roots, grasses, and other natural materials. Some were woven, others coiled. Basketwork made by New Mexico Indians was also used for fences, fish nets, houses, mats, shields, cradles and other items. Anasazi baskets were woven so tightly almost no water would leak from them. Because of dry climate, well-preserved examples of ancient baskets have been found by archaeologists.

Basketmakers

Early Anasazi peoples. This first phase of their culture began around 100 B.C. and lasted about 800 years. They mastered weaving, making baskets from rushes, grasses and vines. Around A.D. 500 they began to live in villages; some villages had 100 houses. The pit-houses were partly underground, in many shapes.

Bat Cave

Along New Mexico's western plains, ears of corn that date back to 3500 B.C. have been found here.

Bandelier National Monument

Ancient dwellings here are carved out of volcanic rock and combined with brick building. See the large 400-room Tyuonyi ruins, several well-preserved kivas, a talus house, the Long House ruins, and the Ceremonial Cave. The Shrine of the Stone Lions is still a place of worship for Pueblo Indians.

C is for . . .

Chief

Leader of a tribe. Different titles meant different things. Some members were made chief because they owned deeds to land. Chieftainship was often inherited, usually from the mother!

Calumet

Also called "peace pipe" or "war pipe." Refers to the stem of the pipe, which is decorated with feathers or carved to signal the tribe's intentions. New Mexico Indians believed the calumet to have great power.

Contact Period

What historians call the era in the 1500s when Native Americans first met Europeans. This meeting changed the lifestyle of the New Mexico Indians more than anyone could ever have anticipated!

Chaco Culture National Historical Park:

One of the most important archaeological sites in North America. Preserves the ruins of the Anasazi. More than 2,000 prehistoric ruins are located within 32 square miles. Also 11 major pueblos and 400 smaller archaeological sites. As many as 5,000 Anasazi may once have inhabited the canyon.

Comanche

Famous Indian tribe of the Plains. Expert horsemen. Famous horse breeders and trainers with huge herds. Buffalo hunters and warlike. Roamed much of the Plains, including New Mexico, in the 1700 and 1800s.

Classical Period of the Anasazi

The era in which this culture built their cities; 900-1300 A.D. The most spectacular ones in our state were in Aztec and Chaco canyons in northwestern New Mexico. These multistoried cliff dwellings were made of sandstone bricks.

Citizenship

The Indian Citizenship Act of 1924 states all Indians born in the United States are citizens of the United States, and citizens of the states they live in, even though they may live on a reservation. They can vote. They pay most local, state and federal taxes, including sales taxes.

Cochise

Famous Chiricahua Apache chief who led the revolt of his tribe against the whites in the 1860s. He was retaliating for injustices the Apache received from the whites and the U.S. Army. Attacked and eluded the U.S. Army for more than 10 years with only 200 followers!

Clan

A tribal unit. Members are descended from the same ancestor.

D is for . . .

Dance

There were Indian dances for every occasion: war, peace, hunting, rain, good harvests, etc. Drums, rattles, and flutes of bone or reed provided the music. Dancers often chanted or sang while performing. Steps were not easy to learn and required consistent practice.

Descendants

The first New Mexico Indians were descendants of primitive hunters who crossed the Bering Strait from Asia to what is now Alaska. At that time, glacial ice still covered most of North America. These people were the true discoverers of the "New World!"

Disease

New Mexico Indians had no immunity to the diseases that white explorers, colonists and settlers brought to their lands. These diseases included smallpox, measles, tuberculosis and others, which ravaged the tribes in great epidemics that killed many, and sometimes all, members of a tribe.

Drought?

For some unknown reason, but probably a drought and/or warfare, the Anasazi culture began to die out in the late 1200s to early 1300s. Scientists believe a great drought may have forced the Anasazi to leave their cities to search for food, and/or more aggressive hunting and gathering tribes (ancestors of the Navajos and Apaches) may have entered their cities to raid them for food.

Dyes

Made of lichens, berries, roots, bark, plants, and other natural materials by Indians in New Mexico. Different colors were used depending on what materials were available and what objects were to be dyed.

Did You Know About These Exciting Events?

Institute of American Indian Arts Spring Pow-wow – April, Santa Fe; Annual Apple Blossom Contest Pow Wow – April, Farmington; Annual Gathering of Nations – April, Albuquerque; Annual Taos Pueblo Pow Wow – July, Taos Pueblo; Annual Santa Fe Indian Market – August, Santa Fe; Annual Jicarilla Apache Go-Jii-Ya – September, Stone Lake; Annual Sky City Powwow – September, Acoma Pueblo

Dreams

Important in the Indian tradition. It was believed that dreams were the "windows" to the soul. Many thought a person's hidden desires were expressed in dreams.

E is for . . .

Eagle

An animal used in many Indian ceremonies. Eagle feathers attached to war bonnets and shields communicated an Indian's rank in his tribe and what kinds of deeds he had done. Feathers also adorned rattles, pipes, baskets, and prayer sticks.

El Morro

Massive sandstone mesa located in the Navajo Indian Reservation in northwestern New Mexico. Site of the ruins of the Atsinna pueblo. Nearby is 200-foot-high Inscription Rock, where, since ancient times, peoples have stopped to carve drawings or words. The name means "the bluff." Made a national monument in 1906.

Enchanted Mesa

Legendary home of the Acoma people. Rises about 400 feet from the plains a few miles east of Acoma.

Environment

Preserving the environment is important to preserving Native American heritage. For thousands of years, Native American tribes lived completely off the land. Farming, mining, pollution have all had a part in changing native environments.

Earrings

Medicine men sometimes pierced male and female ears at special ceremonies. Earrings, which cost parents or relatives a significant amount, symbolized wealth and distinction. The more earrings that an Indian wore, the greater his honor. Some earrings measured 12 inches in length!

English

In the 1800s, the U.S. government built boarding schools for Indian children throughout the nation. Children were forced to leave their homes and families to live at these schools. They were required to learn English and not speak their native languages.

Epidemics

Few Indians possessed immunity to the deadly diseases, like smallpox and measles, which European explorers and settlers brought to the New World. As a result, great population loss took place. Sometimes entire tribes became extinct. Epidemics sparked by Hernando De Soto's expedition are estimated to have killed 75% of the native population in the New World.

F is for . . .

Fetish

These small objects were thought to hold the spirit of an animal or a part of nature. A fetish could be an object found in nature, such as bone or wood, or it could be a carved object. The fetish was usually small enough to be carried in a small bag or on a cord. The making and use of a fetish was kept secret by its owner and only shared with the one who inherited it.

"Fearing Time"

What the Navajo Indians called the terrible 4 years they were forced to spend on the Bosque Redondo reservation. During this time, at least 2,000 starved to death or died of disease.

Fort Union National Monument

Established in 1851. Largest fort in the Southwest at the time, built to guard the Santa Fe Trail. Also was the staging area for operations against the Ute, Jicarilla, Apache, Comanche and Kiowa Indians.

Fire Drill

A device used by Indians to make fires which consisted of a stick and a piece of wood with a tight hole in it. The stick was twirled rapidly in the hole, creating friction that would ignite shredded grass or wood powder placed nearby to start a fire.

Farmers

Many New Mexico Indians, ancient and modern, have farming ways! Even pre-contact Indians tilled and irrigated, raising many important crops. Corn, cotton, beans, squash, melons, sunflowers, gourds, pumpkins and tobacco are all native Indian crops!

Federal Recognition

The United States government's official acknowledgement of a group of Indians as a tribe that is eligible for government benefits, programs and funds.

Footwear

New Mexico Indians wore different footwear depending on their tribe and environment. Moccasins were made mostly of animal skin. Sandals were made of rawhide or plant material.

Folsom Museum

See displays related to the discovery by a cowhand of a 10,000-year-old arrowhead embedded in a bison skeleton, including the chipped stone darts known as Folsom points.

G is for . . .

Great Kiva at Aztec Ruins

Has been restored to look like it did when it was used as a ceremonial chamber by the Anasazi.

Games

Adults played ball and other games of chance or skill. Indian children spun tops, fought pretend battles, did target-shooting, walked on stilts, played hide and seek, or competed to see who could hold their breath the longest!

Geronimo

Famous chief of the Chiricahua Apache. His original name meant "One Who Yawns." Born around 1829 near the Arizona/New Mexico border. Fought with Mexican troops starting in 1858, and later American troops. Finally forced to surrender, his band and two others were sent as prisoners of war to Florida where they worked at hard labor until they were relocated to Oklahoma. Became a legend nationwide, attending important national events although he was still a prisoner of war.

Gorgets

Beautiful ornaments hung around the neck or from ears; their significance, if any, is unknown.

Gens

Group of related members from different tribes.

Gathering

Native Americans gathered natural materials for food, fuel, baskets, clothing, and housing. American Indians tribes also hunted to meet basic needs. Even though some tribes planted crops, most did some kind of gathering.

Great Period of the Anasazi

Lasted from 900 to 1300 A.D. Besides building their cities, these peoples traded far and wide and made great progress in art and science. The remains of their incredible buildings astounded the Spanish who saw them. See them today in the Four Corners area. More than 25,000 Anasazi sites have been identified in our state.

Gourds

Hollowed-out shell of a gourd plant's dried fruit which often grew into a specific shape. Indians raised many species of gourds. They were used for spoons, bowls, masks, rattles, and even storage.

Government

The ancient Pueblo people practiced self-government in their cities. They drew their laws from ancient religious commandments. Some scholars say that the magnificent Anasazi life declined when their cities outgrew their old form of government and was not replaced with a new one.

Gila Cliff Dwellings

Located in southwestern New Mexico. Were inhabited by the Mogollon people from about A.D. 1 to 1300. Included 42 rooms in 5 caves about 175-feet above the canyon floor. Located in the Gila National Forest and part of the Gila Cliff Dwellings National Monument.

H is for . . .

Horn and Hooves

Indians used animal horn to make spoons and dishes. Hooves were made into rattles and bird beaks were used for decoration.

Hatchet

A small, short-handled ax, primarily used as a tool, not as a weapon. When settlers moved in, stone hatchets were replaced with iron ones.

Hair

Indians used hair as a textile. Hair from bison, mountain sheep, elk, moose, deer, dog, rabbit, beaver, or even humans were used to weave cloth, make wigs, or stuff pillows, balls, dolls or drumsticks.

Hogan

The hogan is a residence and/or ceremonial dwelling for the Navajo. Originally built with a 5-sided forked-stick log frame. If extra insulation was needed, it might be entirely covered with packed adobe or mud, hiding the faceted shape. The door always faces east towards the rising sun. Six or eight sided hogans are a new style since the early 1900's. The arrival of the railroad brought large supplies of cross-ties, which could be laid horizontally to form walls of a larger, taller hogan. There are two styles of hogans: the male hogan and the female hogan.

Hunters

Early Indian peoples were hunters who used wooden spears with stone points to kill many kinds of large mammals that are extinct today, such as mammoths and mastodons!

Hisatsinom

The name the present-day Southwest Indians usually give to their ancient ancestors. Preferred by them to the Navajo word most commonly used: "Anasazi."

Horses

Spaniards brought the horse to America. At first, Indians were afraid of the horse or thought it was sacred. Later, Indians "broke" horses gently, often "hypnotizing" them with a blanket. Horses were used for transportation, trade, barter or payment. Some Indians ate horse meat in hopes of gaining the animal's power.

Hornos

A traditional outdoor pueblo bread-baking oven that cooks using radiant heat. They are beehive-shaped. The Spanish taught the Pueblos how to build these ovens and bake bread with them in the mid 1500s. Hornos are passed on for generations and are still used today.

I is for . . .

Isleta Pueblo

Tiwa-speaking peoples who once lived here were called Tauweaga or Kick-Flaking Stone People. Today, it has the largest population of any pueblo, with around 3,000 residents.

Indian Pueblo Cultural Center

Albuquerque; includes Pueblo history and craft techniques, explained step-by-step. Traditional Indian dances are also performed here.

Indian Removal Act of 1830

This federal act gave President Andrew Jackson the power to relocate tribes east of the Mississippi to an "Indian Territory." The forced removal of the southeast Indians later became known as the "Trail of Tears."

Independence

Native American tribes are sovereign nations. That means they are independent. Some even issue their own passports! However, Native Americans are also considered citizens of the United States and enjoy all the rights and privileges of U.S. citizens.

Indian Wars

In 1862 the Union army sent Gen. James Carleton to New Mexico to put down the Apache and Navajo Indians. For 4 years he tried to rule as a dictator, refusing to council with the Indians and ordering any Indian men found to be killed. He asked Kit Carson, a mountain man accustomed to dealing with Indians, to help him. In a short time, Carson had defeated the Mescalero Apaches. A few hundred were forced to move to Bosque Redondo, a reservation on the Pecos River. Next, Carson burned the fields, trees and animals of the Navajo Indians. This caused starvation among the Indians, who were too scattered to fight any organized battle and who had no guns to fight with. In 1864, Carson fought the Indians at Canyon de Chelly; he spared the lives of those who surrendered. But 8,000 Indians were forced to march during the bitter winter, with little food or warm clothes, to the reservation at Bosque Redondo. This journey was called the Long Walk.

Indian

In 1493, Christopher Columbus called the native people he met in North America "Indians" because he mistakenly believed he had sailed to India! Today, this term includes the aborigines of North and South America.

Indian Ladder

Indians made ladders by trimming branches off a tree. Some were left at consistent intervals to provide steps.

Indian Tribes in New Mexico

At one time or another, these tribes have lived in the state of New Mexico: Apache, Comanche, Navajo, Tonkawa, Ute, Zuni

J is for . . .

Just So You Know . . .

Today you can find many New Mexico Indians that follow some traditional ways. But there are also many who are entrepreneurs, doctors, lawyers, educators and even politicians! If you visit a reservation or cultural event, make sure you know visitor etiquette. Often dances are religious ceremonies and should be observed as such; religious dances should not be applauded. Photography, videotaping and drawing are all important issues - check with the tribe or individual before any is started.

Jemez Pueblo

Once, 7 villages were located here. The Jemez tribe forced from the pueblo was resettled in Walatowa by the Spanish in 1696. The pueblo was later resettled, and today has close to 1800 residents.

Jewelry

The jewelry that the Anasazi made was magnificent. Some necklaces contained at least 1,000 precisely worked stones!

Jornada del Muerto

Journey of the Dead. What the walk across a scorching desert trail that Spanish survivors of the Pueblo Indian revolt of 1680 had to endure. They gathered at the mission of El Paso del Norte (the present-day Juarez, Mexico.)

Jicarilla Apaches

This group of Apache live on the Jicarilla Reservation in north-central New Mexico. They have nearly one million acres. Here they raise sheep and livestock and operate several lucrative oil and gas wells. The name Jicarilla means "little basket" in Spanish; their native name for themselves is "Tinde."

Just In Time!

The Indian Arts and Crafts Act of 1990 makes it against the law to pretend that an item has been made by Native Americans if it is really not. It is illegal to offer or display for sale, or sell any art or craft product in a way that falsely suggests it is Indian produced.

Jacal

A certain type of native American house built from adobe and wood.

Jemez State Monument

Ruins of the Giusewa pueblo, which was abandoned after the Pueblo Revolt of 1680. See reproductions of frescoes discovered on the church walls in 1920.

K is for . . .

Kachina

Pueblo Indians believes supernatural spirits or gods inhabited the mountains, and that during ceremonial dances, these gods were supposed to visit the village in spirit. The dancers, wearing masks, represented these gods. Wood dolls, dressed like the dancers, were used to instruct children. There are more than 100 kinds of kachinas.

Kill Site

An archaeological site where remains of many animals have been found along with human artifacts. Many kill sites have been useful to scientists in learning how ancient American Indians lived.

Kiva

Sunken ceremonial chamber; built partly underground and entered through the roof by ladders.

Knife

Made from various materials such as bone, reed, stone, wood, antler, shell, metal, or animal teeth (bear, beaver, etc.), knives were used as weapons but also creative handiwork.

Killed Pottery

Pottery placed in a grave as an offering to the dead person was called killed pottery. A hole was formed in its base during creation. Often broken pottery was placed in a grave because Indians believed the spirit of the dead person would then be released and could travel.

K'hapoo

Means "where the wild roses grow." Original name of the Santa Clara Pueblo. Early Tewa inhabitants joined other Indians on the nearby Black Mesa to protest the murder of Indians by Spanish for practicing their traditional religion.

Kuana

Multistoried Rio Grande pueblo of 1,200 rooms, now part of the Coronado State Monument. One of the 12 Tiguex pueblos located on the west bank of the river. Built about 1325 and populated until the Spanish forced many pueblos to be consolidated. A restored kiva with reconstructed frescoes can be seen here.

Knots

Tied on bowstrings, spearhead and arrowhead lashings, snowshoes, and other items, knots were sometimes used to keep track of the days like a calendar—each knot equaled 1 day.

Keresan Pueblo

Indians of an independent stock, having no connection with any other. Generally called Pueblo Indians. Still live on the Rio Grande, in north-central New Mexico.

L is for . . .

Linguistic Families

There are 56 related groups of American Indian languages. A few of these speech families include Iroquoian, Algonquian, Siouan, Muskogean, Athapascan, and Wakashan.

Leggings

Both men and women wore cloth or skin covering, which were often decorated with quills, beads, or painted designs, for their legs.

Lost Tribes of Israel

This historic theory has been floating around since 721 BC. The 10 lost tribes of Israel are supposedly groups of people gathered together by Sargon, the King of Assyria. Some say he cast out 10 of the 12 tribes of Israel. Many have tried to prove that the American Indians are these missing tribes!

Long Walk

The tragic 1864 journey of the Navajo Indians who were forced to give up their homelands and resettle on a reservation. Hundreds of men, women and children died along the 300-mile trail because of the bitter cold, lack of food, minimal clothing and disease.

Lodge

The term for a type of Indian house that was usually a permanent dwelling. The population of a tribe was often estimated by its number of lodges.

Land Loss

Native Americans lost their land in many ways. Conflicts with other tribes, colonization, European settlement, treaties, and removal took away Indian lands.

Lance

Spear used for hunting and war. The hunting lance had a short shaft and a broad, heavy head. The war lance was light and had a long shaft.

Laguna Pueblo

Near Albuquerque. Although evidence shows people living here since the 1300s, the pueblo became officially recognized by the Spanish in 1699. The people were refugees from many tribes fleeing the Spanish reconquest of New Mexico. Made up of 6 villages spread out around the original settlement, Old Laguna.

Lariat

These throw ropes made of rawhide, buffalo hair, or horsehair sometimes measured up to 20 feet long!

M is for . . .

Maize

Also called Indian Corn. Known as a "cereal" plant because it probably began as some form of grass. The Indians in our state figured out every possible way to use corn as a food. The only thing the white man added was the creation of "corn flakes!"

Mortar and Pestle

A two-part milling tool, with a bowl-shaped stone, plus a club-shaped stone (or wooden bowl and wooden club), used for pulverizing or grinding plants or animal matter.

Metate and Mano

The Anasazi mortar and pestle used to grind corn.

Medicine

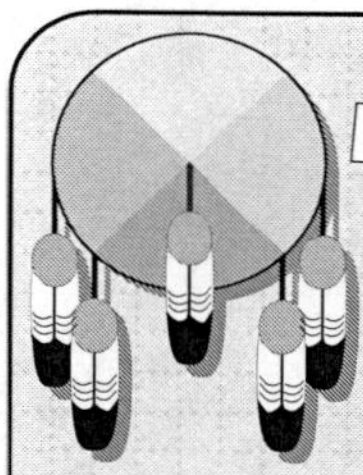

Medicine could be good or bad. Medicines or charms were placed in a bag by young warriors and carried at all times. Some of the roots, leaves and bark that Indians in our state used as medicine are being rediscovered and used by today's doctors!

Moccasins

Indian shoes made of animal skin.

Medicine Man

A person who got the power to heal the sick through a secret means, usually from a dream or visions.

Mogollon

Ancient New Mexico culture. They were the first people in the southwest to build houses, farm and make pottery. They appeared in the southern part of the state near the Arizona border about 2,000 years ago. These people also built villages, worshiped at large communal lodges, and made woven baskets. For generations they were the cultural leaders of the Southwest.

N is for . . .

Nomadic

A way of life in which people frequently moved from one location to another in search of food. "Seminomadic" people had permanent villages, but left them in certain seasons to hunt, fish, or gather wild plant foods.

Nomadic Indians

The so-called nomadic groups of peoples (which refers more to the fact that they once roamed the land) include the Jicarilla Apaches, the Mescalero Apaches, the Utes and the Navajos. Most of these peoples live on reservations today.

Nation

There are many Indian nations located within the United States, such as the Zuni Nation. Indian nations are called nations because their governments and laws are independent of and separate from the U.S. government. The federal government must have "government to government" relations with these Indian nations, just as it would with foreign nations, like England or Spain.

Nahondzod

Means "Fearing Time;" what the Navajo called the time they spent at Bosque Redondo from 1864-1868.

November

In 1990, President George Bush approved a joint resolution designating November 1990 "National American Indian Heritage Month." Similar proclamations have been issued each year since 1994.

Names

Indian names were often changed during one's lifetime. These names could be derived from events that happened during the person's birth, childhood, adolescence, war service, or retirement from active tribal life. Some names came from dreams, some were inherited, and sometimes names were stolen or taken in revenge. Today some Indians maintain old, traditional Indian names, while others take modern names. Since settlers often did not read or write Indian languages, they recorded Indian names phonetically (as they "sounded"). Thus Indian names were often misspelled.

Navajo

America's largest Native American group, which includes over 250,000 people. Once lived a nomadic life, wandering over an enormous land area. Today they live on a reservation of 18.4 million acres, which spills over into Arizona and Utah. This is the largest Indian reservation in the U.S. These Indians pursue mining, lumber, power and and agricultural enterprises. Master craftsmen, they also make and sell beautiful silver items, baskets and sandpaintings. World-famous for their woven blankets and rugs.

National Museum of the American Indian

The Smithsonian's National Museum of the American Indian on the National Mall in Washington, D.C., symbolizes a deeper understanding between America's first citizens and those who have come to make these shores their home.

O is for . . .

Old Bones

No one knows for sure when the first people came to North America, but scientists have dated bones and artifacts discovered at Clovis, New Mexico around 11,200 years old. Testing on a skeleton found on the Channel Islands, off the coast of California showed they were about 13,000 years old. And, evidence of human habitation in southern New Mexico suggests that people may have been there as far back as 38,000 years ago.

Old Town

Tiwa-speaking Indians occupied a pueblo on this site as early as 1350. Today, the city-center of Albuquerque.

Origins

Some scientists believe that Native Americans actually came across a land bridge between Asia and North America. They say that during an ice age thousands of years ago, the water level was much lower and people could have walked between the two continents.

Oil

Indians extracted oil from the many layers of fat that came with fresh bear meat. The fat was boiled down in earthen pots to produce the oil, which was stored in gourds and pots. The oil was used for cooking and even beautifying the body! Indians would mix red pigment with the oil, add the fragrances of cinnamon and sassafras, and rub it all over their bodies.

Oldest House

Located in Santa Fe; possibly the oldest house in the United States. Made of adobe walls of poured mud instead of bricks. Foundations may have been built by Pueblo Indians in the 13th century.

Orators

Many Indian leaders were excellent public speakers. Powerful and dramatic speakers were vital to leaders who wanted to influence their tribe. Watch for famous Indian quotations in literature and textbooks!

Office of Indian Education Programs

This is a service organization devoted to providing quality education opportunities for American Indian people. Established in the latter part of the nineteenth century to carry out the federal government's education commitment to Indian tribes, it has become the only national education system for American Indian children and adults.

P is for . . .

Powwow

The original form of the word meant "medicine man." Medicine men would often use noise motion and confusion to scare away harmful spirits and cure people. It was also a gathering to talk about political matters. Today, the powwow is an event where Indians gather to sing, perform ceremonial dances, and share cultural pride and traditions.

Petroglyph State Park

Known as the West Mesa; 17-mile serpentine stretch of volcanic rock. Contains 15,000 prehistoric pictures made of white or gray lines chipped into the dark rock by the Anasazi and Tiwa.

Puye Cliff Dwellings

On top of Pajarito Plateau; between A.D. 600 and 1580 houses were located for more than a mile.

Pecos

Indian tribe that occupied the largest and most populous pueblo in historic times. Only 17 Pecos, whose descendants still live, survived enemy Indian raids.

Paint

Indians used many natural materials to make paint, like clay mixed with oil or grease. Yellow "paint" was made with the gall bladder of a buffalo! Why did they paint their faces or bodies? Indians used paint to look scary or beautiful, to disguise themselves, or to protect their skin from sunburn or insect bites. Indians often applied red paint because it symbolized strength and success. That is why settlers often referred to the Indians as Red Men.

Popé

San Juan Pueblo leader of the Pueblo Revolt in 1680. He had been imprisoned and publicly whipped rather than denounce his traditional Indian religion. While he led the people to victory, it did not last long. The Indians began to quarrel among themselves, then went their separate ways.

Pueblo Indians

When Spaniards first came to the American Southwest, they found some Indians lived in towns, while others were nomadic. They called these village-dwellers pueblos after the Spanish word for towns. Pueblos were not a single tribe, but several groups of people who shared a common culture, but not necessarily a common language. The Pueblo people of the Southwest have lived in the same location longer than any other culture in the United States! Nineteen pueblo groups live in New Mexico today. Their towns are also called pueblos and look much as they did centuries ago. These pueblos are Acoma, Cochiti, Isleta, Jemez, Laguna, Nambe, Picuris, Pojoaque, Sandia, San Felipe, San Ildefonso, San Juan, Santa Ana, Santa Clara, Santo Domingo, Taos, Tesuque, Zia and Zuñi.

Pottery

Indian pottery was made from built-up spirals of clay that were molded or paddled, or a combination of the two methods. Used as cooking or storage vessels. New Mexico Indians are known for some of the finest pottery!

Q is for . . .

Quillwork

Indians used the quills of porcupine or birds to make a type of embroidery. Quills were dyed with juice from berries and other materials. When they were ready to be used, the quills were either mashed with teeth or softened with hot water and flattened with rocks. The quills were then laced into moccasins, shirts, pipe covers, and other items. Beads which Indians received by trading with settlers eventually replaced quillwork.

Quality

Native American arts and crafts are known for their excellent craftsmanship and striking designs. This work is often influenced by things found in nature especially plants and animals.

Quarai

In 1980, Grand Quivira National Monument and two state monuments, Abo and Quarai, were combined as the Salinas Pueblo Missions National Monument. Salinas means "salt mines" in Spanish, named for nearby salt deposits. All were large Indian pueblos before the Spanish arrived. The Spanish consolidated many pueblos here, trying to control and rule the Indians more easily. Drought, disease, fighting with the Spanish and Indian attacks eventually drove the Quarai from their homes.

Quiver

Case used to hold arrows; made of woven plant materials or animal skins.

Quarry Site

A location where Indians went for workable stone such as flint and made stone tools.

Quirt

A short riding whip with a wood, bone, or horn handle.

R is for . . .

Rain Dancing

The rain dance ceremony, performed to encourage rainfall, was common among Indian religions because good weather is vital for a successful harvest. Rainmakers were in tune with nature; there are actual reported cases of Indians producing or preventing rain!

Roots

Indians used plant roots for food, medicine, dye, baskets, cloth, rope, salt, flavoring, and just to chew!

Rattles

Indians of New Mexico made rattles from bird beaks, animal hooves, bones, pods, seashells, turtle shells and other animal parts. The rattles are used in ceremonies.

Ruins

You can see some amazing ruins at Aztec Ruins National Monument, in Aztec. They are some of the largest and best-preserved Anasazi ruins in the Southwest. The West Ruins have 450 interconnected rooms. The roof of the Great Kiva may have weighed 95 tons when originally built!

Rawhide

Untanned animal hide. The "green" hide was stretched on the ground or over a frame. Flesh and fat were removed. The skin was dried, washed, then buried with wood ashes which made the hair come off. Used by the New Mexico Indian to make drumheads, lash lodge poles, mend broken objects and in many other ways.

Reservations

The U.S. government set aside, or "reserved," land for the Indians. These reservations originally served as a sort of prison during the beginning stages of Indian removal. At that time, reservations provided the government with some control over Indian activity and residency. This land was usually considerably less desirable land than the Indians' native territories. Today's reservations are lands that are tribally held, yet protected by the government.

Ruins - Some More!

Pecos National Historic Park includes the large Anasazi Pecos pueblo built around 1300. Served as a center for trade between the Plains and Pueblo peoples. From here, an Indian called the Turk led Coronado in search of the fabled city of Quivira; the Indians hoped the explorer would die or become lost on the wild goose chase!

S is for . . .

Sundial

In 1977, something like a "sundial" was discovered in New Mexico. It was built on a mesa near Chaco Canyon-probably by the Anasazi. The sundial was made of huge stone slabs that let slices of sunlight strike circular lines. By reading the position of the light along the lines, an Anasazi priest would be able to predict the seasons, letting farmers know the best time to plant and harvest their crops.

Salmon Ruin

Near Bloomfield; an over 150-room pueblo. Built in the late 1000s, occupied by various cultures through the late 1200s.

Secret Societies

Indians had secret groups, usually organized for religious or ceremonial reasons. Each society had a purpose, such as to cure disease.

Shield

A piece of "armor" made of a rawhide-covered frame, which was carried into battle. Shields also could be decorative and religious objects. Many tribes make shields today as an art form!

Sweatlodge

Structure used for ritual purification by sweating from exposure to very hot fires or hot steam from pouring water over hot stones. Also called a sweathouse, for some tribes also doubling as clubhouses.

Stone-boiling

Cooking method by placing preheated stones into cooking vessels.

Sacred Bundles

A group of objects treasured by a tribe. They were well-guarded and often taken into battle. The items were publicly shown only on very important occasions.

Signals

Indian signs made with a pony, blanket, mirror, smoke, fire-arrow or other item to communicate over long distances.

Sand Painting

A form of ceremonial art practiced by Indians of the Southwest. The Navajo claim the Cliff Dwellers sand painted only during religious services. The 5 sacred colors of Navajo mythology were used: white, yellow and red were made of powdered sand; black was powdered charcoal, and blue/gray was white sand plus charcoal. Each color had a meaning.

Sandia Mountains

Near Albuquerque archaeologists have uncovered a cave dwelling holding human artifacts that may be as much as 20,000 years old. Some scientists believe that the American Southwest is the most ancient human-settled site in the Western Hemisphere!

Saddle

While some Indians did use saddles on their horses, most rode bareback!

T is for . . .

Tobacco

A sacred plant early Indians used to make offering to their gods, cure diseases, bring good luck, seal agreements and bind treaties.

Treaties

Written agreements between the U. S. government and the Indians, most of which involved the Indians giving up their native lands.

Tonkawa

Before this tribe's removal to Indian Territory, they were known as skilled hunters and fierce raiders who roamed the southern plains of New Mexico, Texas, and Oklahoma.

Totem

The spirit of some natural object (usually an animal) taken by an Indian, tribe or family to guard over them.

Three Rivers Petroglyph Site

More than 500 picture images have been chiseled into the volcanic rock here along the base of the Sacramento Mountains. The designs were made between 900 and 1400 by the Jornada branch of the Mogollon people.

Tomahawk

A club, axe or hammer used to chop wood, drive stakes in the ground or as a weapon.

Tracking

To follow a trail by finding a sign such as a broken blade of grass, a moved stone or moccasin track. Indians learned to trail as children, so that they could find food, track enemies and disguise their own signs.

Teeth

New Mexico Indians hung teeth on cords to make necklaces.

Taos Pueblo

This multistoried pueblo is one of the oldest, most traditional and picturesque of New Mexico's 19 Indian pueblos. The Pueblo Revolt was led from here. In the 1700s, settlers and Indians joined forces to protect themselves from the Ute, Comanche and Navajo, after they kidnapped 50 women and children. Pursuing Spanish soldiers killed 400 Indians in retaliation. Artisans here produce drums, woven textiles and pottery with a glittering mica finish.

Tribe

A group of Indians with shared culture, history, original territory, ancestry, social organization, and governmental structure. A tribe may contain several bands of Indians.

Thunderbird

A mythological Indian figure, as well as a part of the constellations for many Indians. Thunderbird mythology is mostly different from tribe to tribe, in general either coexisting with ancestors as an actual bird, or appearing as a spiritual nature god. The Thunderbird was good to the people in either case. Much mythology ties the thunderbird with thunder, lightning and storms.

U is for . . .

Unique

Each and every tribe has its own unique customs, language, and traditions.

U.S. Army

Many Native Americans have fought bravely for the United States Army. Many have also given their lives for a country that was not always accepting of them.

U.S. Bureau of Indian Affairs

Provides public services such as law enforcement, land records, economic development, and education to Indians. Known for mismanagement and ethical problems.

Ute

These former nomadic New Mexico Indians live along the state's northern border, although the majority live in Utah and Colorado. Once had a custom of handing over all female prisoners to their own women to be tortured!

U.S. Indian Schools

The Bureau of Indian Affairs operates hundreds of federal schools around the nation. Enrollment of Native American children measures in the thousands!

U.S. Indian Reorganization Act

Passed by Congress in 1934, the act authorized Indian tribes to establish and conduct their own governments, and to form businesses.

U.S. Colonists

Called Long Knives or Big Knives by early Indians, who also called English explorers "Coat Men."

U.S. President

Once called Great White Father by Indians.

U.S. Indian Wars

The U.S. War Department has compiled an official list of "Indian Wars" that occurred in the United States. Over 50 wars were fought between the U.S. and the Indians during the period of 1790-1850.

V is for . . .

Vessels

Indians carried water in special gourds shaped liked bottles, called water vessels.

Village Councils

These were held in the town (council) house and occurred to discuss and decide important matters. Harmony and agreement was essential to tribal unity. Rather than vote on issues, they were discussed until everyone was satisfied. Anyone who wanted to could speak freely. Everyone did not always agree on the outcome, but everyone avoided conflict by pushing their case.

Vegetable Dyes

Indians could not buy color from the store like we can today. Instead, they created many different colors from the things they found on earth like plants, flowers, shrubs, trees, roots, and berries. They made beautiful and unique reds, oranges, yellows, greens, browns, and violets. These dyes were used for baskets, pottery, weaving, body makeup, and clothing.

Very Hungry

There were Indians who here hunters, gatherers and foragers, that often ate whatever they could find! How hungry would you have to be to eat what they sometimes ate: reptiles, larvae, and insects?

Villages

Many New Mexico Indians lived in villages! Villages were formed around different clans or bands within the tribe, but could also contain different clans living together. Villages were usually permanent settlements, although semi-nomadic tribes have been known to migrate between permanent villages.

Vesperic Indians

Indian tribes located in the United States.

W is for . . .

War Bonnet

Special headdress worn into battle, often adorned with feathers.

War Pony

Horse, often painted with colorful paint and ridden into battle.

Weavers

The ancient Anasazi peoples wove fine cotton cloth adorned with bright pictures. This southwestern native people's tradition continues today - the Navajo are some of the best-known southwestern weavers.

Wheelwright Museum of the American Indian

Santa Fe; captures the spirit of a Navajo hogan; see sand painting rendered in tapestries and watercolors by a medicine man.

Whistle

Indians from New Mexico made them from the wing bones of birds. The whistles made the sound of the bird the bones came from! Used to communicate, signal, sound an alarm or even flirt with a maiden!

White Man

Indians generally called them Pale Face, a name the white men themselves suggested!

War Club

A weapon made of stone, bone, or wood in the shape of a club.

War Dance

Indian braves danced this before going into battle. The dance was a way of assembling the braves and getting them to commit to the fight ahead.

X Y Z are for . . .

Xenophobe

A xenophobe is someone who is afraid of foreign people, their customs and cultures, or foreign things. Many of the first European settlers were afraid of Native American cultures.

You Bet!

Some Native Americans say that Casinos make a lot of money. Others say that too many people have a gambling problem. In the 1980s and 1990s, many tribes discussed whether or not gambling casinos should be allowed. Now that many casinos have been built across the country, the debate has switched to how it should be controlled.

Zuñi

Indians famous for the silversmithing and the fetishes they carve. A small Zuñi village was probably the first pueblo ever seen by whites. An agricultural people. Grew corn, domesticated the turkey and raised cotton for weaving.

Zuñi Pueblo

Largest of the Indian pueblos. One of the Seven Cities of Cibola that Coronado was looking for, only to find a regular adobe pueblo. The Zuñi today occupy a modern village around the old pueblo of Halona.

ZZZZZZ...

Shamans and medicine men were not the only people who had access to the spirit world. Indians believed that people could make contact with spirits every night in their dreams! Dreamers could travel back to the time of man's creation or far ahead into their own futures. They also believed that dreams contained warnings or commands from the spirits. Many tribes felt that they had to act out their dreams as soon as they awoke. If an Indian dreamed about bathing, for example, he would run to his neighbors' houses first thing in the morning, and his neighbors would throw kettles full of cold water over him.

Y... Or, "Why?"

1. Why do you think Indian warriors carried charms with them? Some Indian medicines have been scientifically proven to have true healing power and are still used today. Do you think their charms had any real power to help them win battles?
2. Why do you think the American government kept relocating Indians onto reservations and then making the reservations smaller and smaller?
3. Why did Indians use items such as a pipe in ceremonies? What kinds of symbolic objects do we use in ceremonies today?
4. Why and how did Indians use natural materials in creative ways?
5. Many Indian tribes are running successful businesses on their reservations today. There is one industry that many tribes are making a lot of money at. Do you know what this is? Hint: "I'll bet you do!"

Which Famous Native American Am I?

Solve the puzzle!

Word Bank

Black Elk	Crazy Horse	Sitting Bull	Sequoia
Sacajawea	Chief Joseph	Geronimo	Pocahontas

Down

1. This Shoshone woman joined Lewis and Clark as their guide and translator and helped make the expedition a success! Hint: She has 4 "a"s in her name!
4. This man gave the Cherokee their first alphabet so that they could write. Until then, they communicated only by speaking and drawing pictures. Hint: A famous ancient tree also has the same name!
5. He was one of the fiercest of Indian warriors! He fought against white settlers in Arizona and New Mexico to keep his people from being pushed off their lands. Hint: Jump!

Across

2. A legend says that this brave Algonquian woman saved the life of Englishman John Smith. Hint: Disney produced a movie about her.
3. He fought at Little Bighorn when he was only 13! He was also a wise "shaman" who saw visions and could advise people. Hint: Part of his name is an animal with antlers!
6. He was a great Sioux warrior who won the battle against General Custer at Little Bighorn in 1876. Hint: His horse was not crazy!
7. A leader of the Lakota (Sioux) tribe who lived on the Standing Rock Reservation in North Dakota after the battle of Little Bighorn. He tried to make conditions better for his people there, so the U.S. government called him a "troublemaker." Hint: He did not sit all the time!
8. A wise and brave chief of the Nez Percé who tried to bring his people to Canada to escape war. He said, "From where the sun now stands, I will fight no more forever." Hint: His father's name was "Old Joseph."

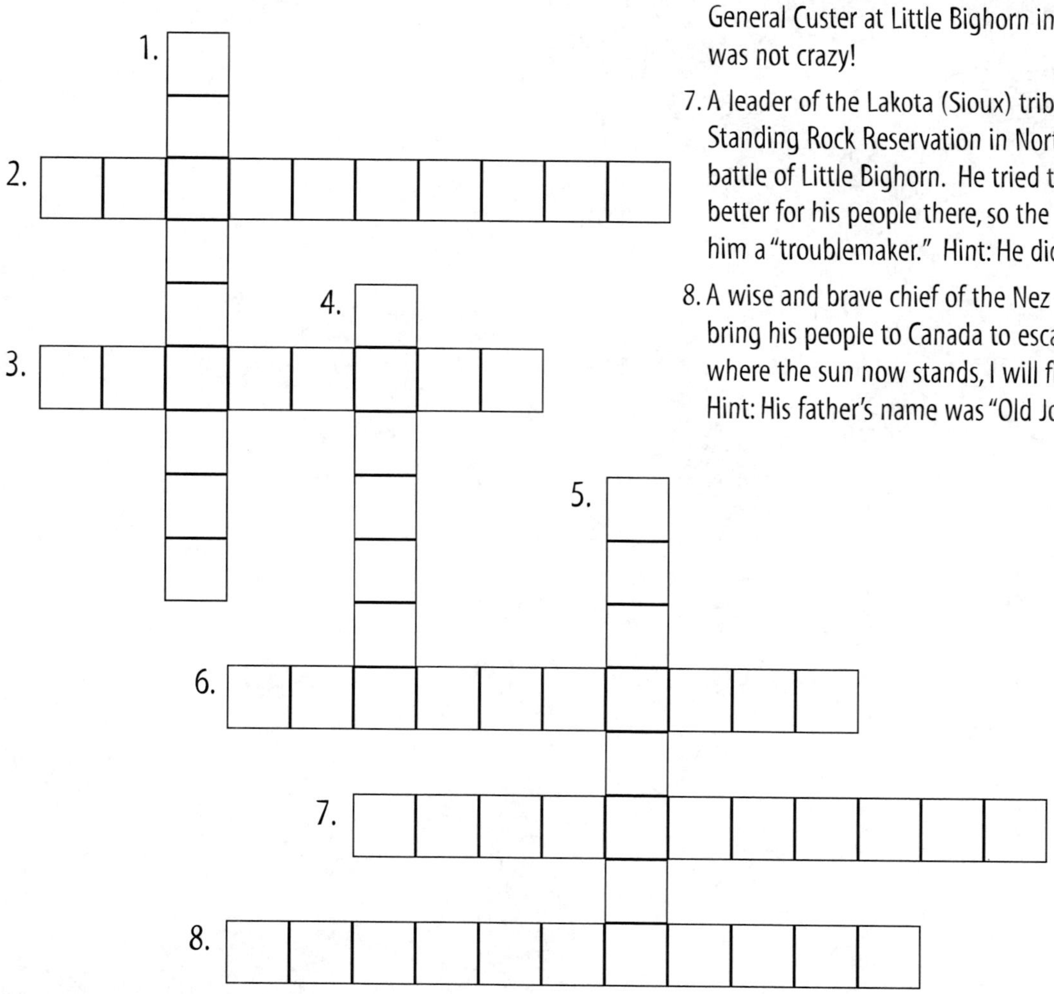

Answer Key: 1. Sacajawea; 2. Pocahontas; 3. Black Elk; 4. Sequoia; 5. Geronimo; 6. Crazy Horse; 7. Sitting Bull; 8. Chief Joseph

Different Ways for Different Indians!

North American Indian tribes are divided into different areas. In each of these areas, tribes shared common ways of living with each other. They might make similar arts or crafts, they might eat the same foods, or they might have had the same beliefs. These activities are all part of their "culture." Each area had its own culture, which was different from the tribes in all the other areas.

Below is a map of all the different groups of Indian tribes in North America. Color each area with a different color. You will see a colorful picture of how Native Americans can all be called "Indians" but still have very different cultures!

Celebration!

Powwows are big festivals where Native Americans gather to sing, dance, and eat together. It is a time to celebrate and show pride in their culture. Powwows can last from one afternoon to several days. The Indians dress in native costumes and dance ancient dances to the beating of drums.

Artists sell their arts and crafts. You might be able to buy some real Native American food cooked on an open fire. Native Americans go to powwows to be with each other, share ideas, and just have fun! Most powwows are also open to people who are not Indian. It's a great place to learn about Native American culture!

If you went to a powwow this weekend, what do you think you would see? What do you think might NOT be there? Circle the objects you think you would see at a powwow. Put an X through those you probably won't see.

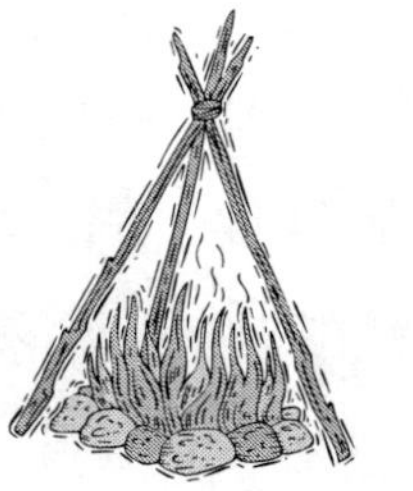

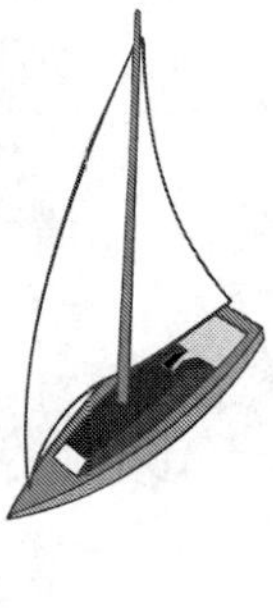

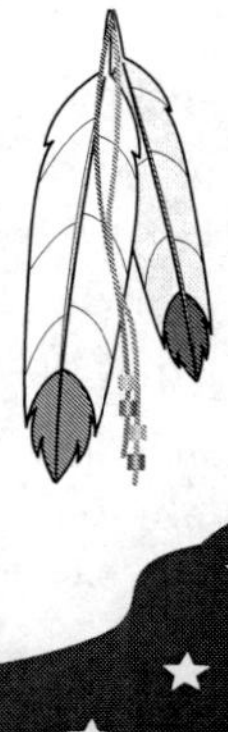

Answer Key: Circled objects are: beads, moccasins, open fire, drums, feathers, baskets, kids, food, drums, horse.

Make an Indian Weaving!

Many Native Americans used weaving to create useful things like sashes (belts), bags, mats, and blankets. They used animal hair to make yarn, and dyed the yarn with natural dyes from fruits and other plants. They also used some plant fibers, like cotton, to make weaving thread.

Weave a small Native American mat of your own. Use different colors of yarn to create a beautiful pattern in your weaving. Place a favorite object on the mat or hang it on your wall!

Prepare the "loom"

Cut a piece of cardboard 5 inches wide and 6 inches long. Along the two 5-inch sides (the "short" sides), have an adult cut slits 1/4 inch deep. These slits should be 1/2 inch apart from each other. So, on each short side you will have 9 slits.

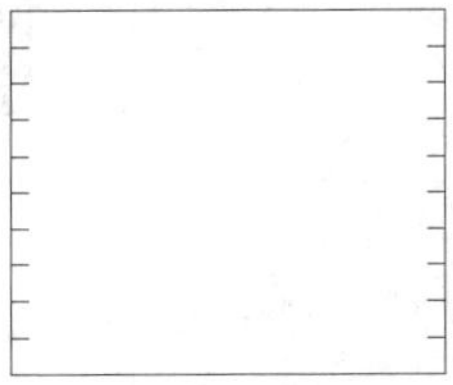

Directions:

1. Take a long piece of yarn and bring it from the back through the first slit (the one next to the edge of the cardboard.) The end of the yarn will hang down behind the cardboard.

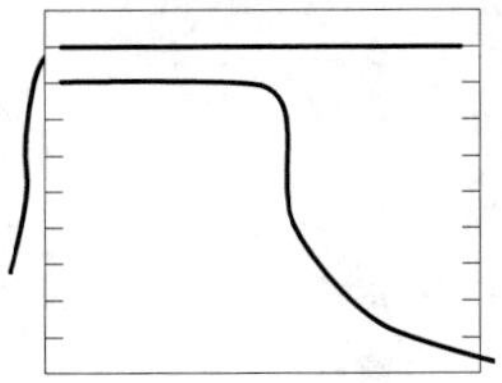

2. Bring the yarn right across the front of the cardboard to the slit opposite the one your yarn came through.

3. Now bring the yarn under the back of the cardboard and then up again through the second slit.

4. Repeat #2 and #3, until you have 9 strands of yarn across the front of your cardboard!

5. Then cut the yarn and tie the two loose ends in the back of the cardboard.

6. Take another piece of yarn and start feeding it through the 9 strands, going over one, under the next over the next, etc. When you get to the end, pull the yarn behind the cardboard and around to the front, and begin again. This time, whatever strand you went over, go under. And whatever strand you went under, go over.

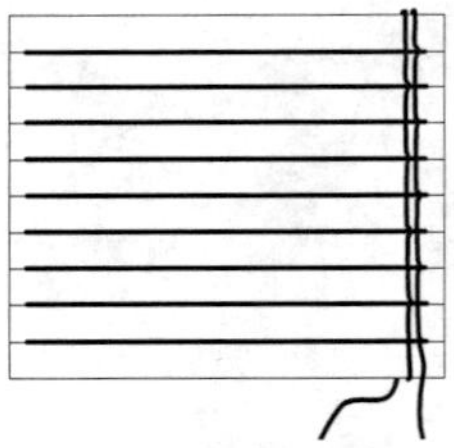

7. Repeat this pattern until the front of your cardboard in covered. Then cut the yarn in the back of the cardboard, and trim it to create a fringe for your mat!

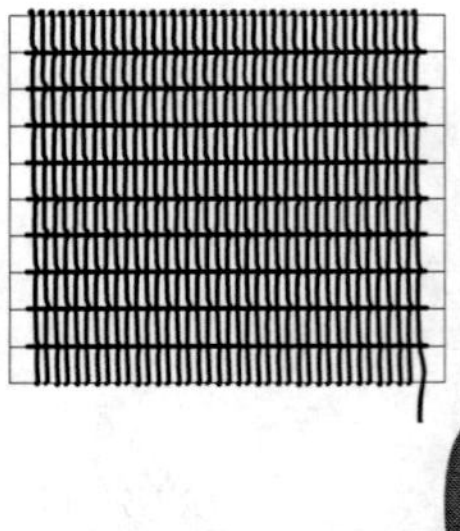

Tips:

- For a wild look, use variegated or different colored yarn!
- For a tighter mat, push the under/over strands up against the previous strands during weaving.
- To keep your mat from unravelling, tie neighboring fringe together up close to the mat.

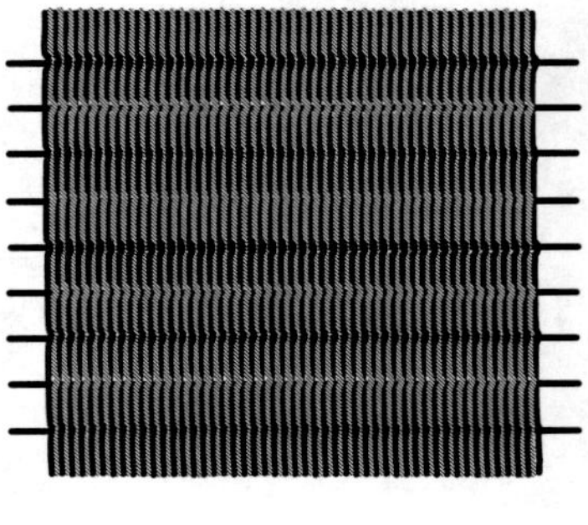

Finders Keepers?

Native Americans have many buried treasures. For hundreds of years, special objects would sometimes be buried with Native Americans, or maybe they would just be lost. Archeologists used to dig for interesting artifacts in old Native American gravesites. They would keep the Native American bones or the arrowheads, rattles, masks and other objects that they found. But this made the Native Americans feel like they were being robbed.

In 1990, the U.S. government passed a law that said that no one could look for or take these Native American objects anymore. And whoever had any already had to give them back to the people they belonged to. This is called repatriation

Help the archeologist return the artifact to a Native American.

Fast Fact

An artifact is an object that was made by people a long time ago for some useful purpose.

Busy Hands!

Before modern times, Native Americans didn't have stores where they went to buy things. They made everything they needed.

What did Indians make with their own hands? Use the Word Bank and pictures to find out!

Word Bank

blanket	moccasins	arrows	pottery	canoe
mat	food	jewelry	pouch	box

___ ___ ___

___ ___ ___ ___

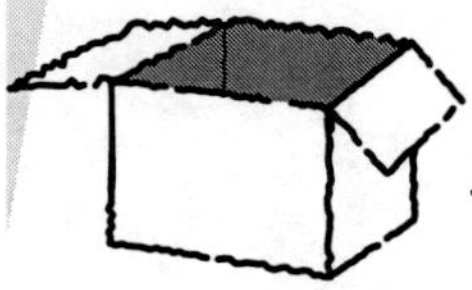
___ ___ ___

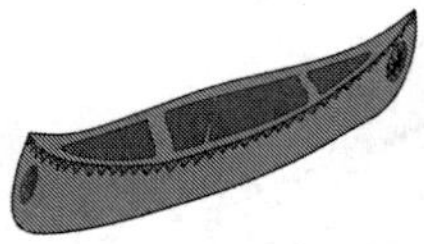
___ ___ ___ ___ ___

___ ___ ___ ___ ___ ___ ___

___ ___ ___ ___ ___

___ ___ ___ ___ ___ ___ ___ ___ ___ ___

___ ___ ___ ___ ___ ___

___ ___ ___ ___ ___ ___ ___

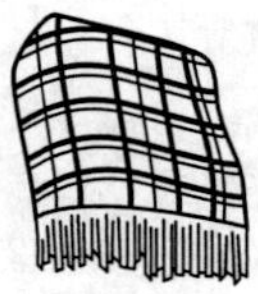
___ ___ ___ ___ ___ ___ ___

American Indians Today

Beginning with the first letter of each group of letters, cross out every other letter to discover some new words. You may not have heard of these before, but you can read all about them!

1. Many Indians live on these, but many more do not!

TRYELSDEBRNVJAOTPIPOWNASX

____

2. Many Indians have been poor for a long time because for many years the government took away their lands and their ability to make a living.

TPKOOVWEBRNTXYA

____

3. Many Indians have been studying hard at school and going to college in order to earn more money. Education helps the Indians make their lives better. These Native Americans are working to become:

TSJUMCBCFEYSMSOFPUVL

____

4. This is a big term that means Native Americans have worked hard to get the U.S. government to let them rule themselves. This means that they have their own laws and make their own decisions. They are like a separate country inside the U.S.! Now, try and see if you can get your parents to give you the same thing!

TSGENLBF **JDGEETSEWRAMCIHNUAKTYIKOTNU**

______________ ______________________________

Fast Fact

What do Indians work as today?

- doctors
- nurses
- factory workers
- artists
- lawyers
- actors

The same kinds of jobs any American might work at!

Native Americans Move to the City!

Solve the code to discover the mystery words!

A	B	C	D	E	F	G	H	I	J	K	L	M
✷	❀	⌘	♣	➧	❤	❗	✰	✂	✆	☛	✈	✉
N	**O**	**P**	**Q**	**R**	**S**	**T**	**U**	**V**	**W**	**X**	**Y**	**Z**
✿	✩	❖	✡	✏	❥	☎	✒	✙	✖	✍	✠	✓

1. During the 1950s and 1960s, the American government paid Indians to leave their homes on reservations and move to cities to get jobs. If cities are sometimes called urban areas, then these brave Indians were called:

✒ ✏ ❀ ✷ ✿   ✂ ✿ ♣ ✂ ✷ ✿ ❥

2. Many Indians chose to stay on their reservations and not move to the city. They thought that if they moved to the city, they would lose the way of life that their parents and ancestors had taught. These Indians called themselves:

✏ ➧ ❥ ➧ ✏ ✙ ✷ ☎ ✂ ✩ ✿   ✂ ✿ ♣ ✂ ✷ ✿ ❥

3. Native Americans who moved to cities lived close to each other. They tried to keep their way of life as much as possible. They did not want to forget their religion, native art, or music. They did not want to lose their:

⌘ ✒ ✈ ☎ ✒ ✏ ➧

4. Are you afraid of heights? Many people are. The Mohawk Indians are not! Many of them work hundreds of feet above the city to build steel frames for skyscrapers. People who do this work above the city are:

❥ ☎ ➧ ➧ ✈   ✖ ✩ ✏ ☛ ➧ ✏ ❥

5. Today urban Indians and reservation Indians come together to celebrate their culture. They share ideas and stories. They dance and beat drums. They make and sell Indian jewelry. During these celebrations, Indians remember how much they have to be proud of! These big parties are called

❖ ✩ ✖ ✖ ✩ ✖ ❥